characters created by
lauren child

YOU
can be my
friend

PUFFIN

Text based on the script written by Carol Noble
Illustrations from the TV animation
produced by Tiger Aspect

PUFFIN BOOKS
Published by the Penguin Group: London, New York, Australia,
Canada, India, Ireland, New Zealand and South Africa
Penguin Books Ltd, Registered Offices: 80 Strand, London WC2R 0RL, England

puffinbooks.com

This edition published in Great Britain in Puffin Books 2012
001 – 10 9 8 7 6 5 4 3 2 1
Text and illustrations copyright © Lauren Child/Tiger Aspect Productions Limited, 2008
Charlie and Lola word and logo ® and © Lauren Child, 2005
Charlie and Lola is produced by Tiger Aspect Productions
All rights reserved
The moral right of the author/illustrator has been asserted
Manufactured in China
ISBN: 978-0-718-19526-7
This edition produced for the Book People Ltd,
Hall Wood Avenue, Haydock, St Helens, WA11 9UL

I have this little sister Lola.
   She is small and very funny.
Today Lola is excited because
   Marv is coming over and he is
bringing his little brother Morten.

Lola says,
"Me and Morten are going to do LOTS
    of things together, like have a tea party!
I LOVE having tea parties.
            And dressing up!

Everyone LOVES dressing up."

Then I say,
"If you run out of things to do,
Morten really likes playing
Round-and-Round."

But Lola says,

"Oh no! I really do not like
Round-and-Round.

All you do is go **round** and **round**...
and **round**. Nothing happens, Charlie."

Then the doorbell rings
and Lola shouts,
"MORTEN'S HERE!"

Lola says, "Hello, Morten."

Morten doesn't say **anything**.

So Marv says,
"Morten's not really a big talker."

And Lola says,
"Morten, do you want to see my room?"

But Morten still doesn't say **anything**.

Lola says,

   "Would you like a cup of tea, Morten?"

         Morten just stares.

So then she asks, "Would you like a biscuit?"

Not a peep from Morten.

"Oh," says Lola.
"Well, what we'll do now is..."

"... **dressing up!**
Look at me, Morten.
I'm a mermaid.

Morten, you can be a **pirate**."

But Morten just stands there.

So Lola says,
      "I know! Let's pretend we live
in Upside Down."

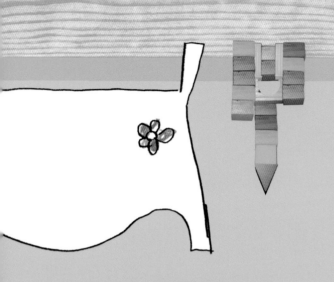

Lola says,
"In Upside Down, absolutely everything is
completely ¡umop ǝp!sdn

Would you like a tea of cup, Morten?
That's Upside Down for 'cup of tea'!"

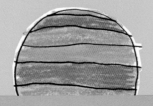

Morten doesn't even move.

So Lola shouts,
"Morten! Don't you want to play?"

Morten just shakes his head.

Later, Lola whispers,
"Morten didn't like any of my gᵃmᵉs, Charlie.
He didn't even talk to me."

So I say,
"Marv told you, Morten isn't really a **big** talker."

Then Lola says,
    "But he didn't even say one SINGLE word.
He doesn't like me."

    Then Lola sighs and blows some
bubbles in her pink milk.

And do you know what? Morten starts **giggling**.
"ᴴᵉᵉ hee hee hee hee hee."

Then Morten tries blowing
pink milk **bubbles**.

Lola and Morten **giggle** some more.

Then Lola says,
"I know! I know!
    Next let's play bubbles outside.

Morten, what do you think it would be like to be inside a bubble?"

"Bubbly," says Morten.

"I looooove being in a **bubble**," says Lola.

And Morten says,
"I love being
in a **bubble**, too."

Later, we all have tea at Marv and
          Morten's flat. Lola and Morten can't
stop **giggling** and **whispering** together.

Morten asks,
"Would you like to play a game, Lola?

It's called **Round-and-Round!**"

Lola looks unsure so I say, "Go on, Lola."

And Lola says, "OK, Charlie. But only because Morten is my new special friend."

Morten says,
"Your turn, Lola! What you do is..."

"I know," says Lola.
"You go round
        and round and round...
    and round."